For Oscar and Leo – S.W.

First published in 2003 by Macmillan Children's Books
A division of Macmillan Publishers Limited
20 New Wharf Road, London N1 9RR
Basingstoke and Oxford
Associated companies throughout the world
www.panmacmillan.com

ISBN 0 333 96221 4 (HB)
ISBN 0 333 99289 X (PB)

Text copyright © 2003 Dyan Sheldon
Illustration copyright © 2003 Sophy Williams

A CIP catalogue record for this book is available from the British Library.

Printed in Belgium by Proost

The Last Angel

DYAN SHELDON

Illustrated by SOPHY WILLIAMS

MACMILLAN CHILDREN'S BOOKS

Heaven was filled with great excitement and joy.
The Son of God was soon to be born in Bethlehem.
Every angel was going to greet Him, from the
very first, the Archangel Michael, to the very last.

The very last angel was Zillah. She was
the last angel because she was always late.
Not only was she always late, but she never quite
managed to do anything as well as the other angels.

Zillah could not fly as fast or as high as the other angels.
She was hopeless at singing and could never find her harp.
But this time Zillah was determined to do everything right.

"You'll see," she said to the Archangel Michael. "When the Baby Jesus
is born, I'm going to bring Him the most wonderful gift of all."

The Archangel Michael smiled.

"And just what is this wonderful gift to be?" he asked.

"Well . . ." Zillah hesitated. "I don't really know yet.
I have to think about it very carefully."

"Just don't think about it for too long," advised Michael,
"or you may not get to Bethlehem at all."

It took Zillah a long time to think of
a perfect gift for the Baby Jesus.
Then, at last, she leapt to her
feet with a smile.

She would bring the
Baby Jesus a crown of stars,
so everyone would know He was
the King of Heaven and Earth.

But by the time Zillah reached the stars,
another angel was floating away with
a shimmering crown.
"I'm sorry, Zillah," said the other angel.
"I'm afraid you're a little late."

"Well, I'll just have to think of something else,"
Zillah said to herself. "Something even better."

It took her quite a while to think of something better
than a crown of stars, but at last she thought of exactly
the right gift and she set off to collect it.

Zillah had decided to make the Baby Jesus
a beautiful, warm blanket from the feathers
of every bird on the Earth.

But there were rather more birds on
the Earth than Zillah had thought.

By the time Zillah returned to Heaven, the other angels
were starting to leave.

"Hurry, Zillah!" called the Archangel Michael.
"We have to get to Bethlehem as quickly as we can!"
Zillah stared back at him in horror. He was carrying his
gift for the Baby Jesus . . . it was a magnificent
blanket made from the feathers of every bird on the Earth!

But Zillah didn't give up. Stuffing her feathers under
a cloud, she hurried after the others. She would find
a gift on the way to Bethlehem.
At least she hadn't been left behind.

The hills of the countryside were covered with snow,
and the night was cold and dark.
    "What will you find for the Baby Jesus out
here?" the other angels worried.

    Zillah, however, was determined.
    "There will be something . . ." she said.
    "I know there will."

As they flew over city after city, Zillah searched for her special gift.
She saw many precious and beautiful things: merchants counting golden coins,
and kings in fine robes, covered with jewels. But Zillah knew that neither gold
nor fine robes, nor even jewels, were special enough for the Son of God.
   Then Zillah looked up – the other angels were far ahead of her!

"Wait for me!" shouted Zillah. "Please wait!"
   But the angels didn't hear her.

Zillah beat her wings as hard as she could.
She tried and tried to fly faster to catch up with the
other angels, but still she fell further behind.
Soon the other angels were no more than a distant blur.
"Oh, no!" wailed poor Zillah. "I'm going to miss
the birth of the Baby Jesus!"
Exhausted, Zillah sat down in the snow and wept.

And then, through her tears, Zillah
saw a tiny flower poking through the snow.
It was as blue as the sky and as fragile as a
butterfly's wings. She could hardly believe it.

If a tiny, fragile flower could force its
way through the snow, then surely she
was strong enough to get to Bethlehem
after all. Wiping her eyes, Zillah
scrambled to her feet.

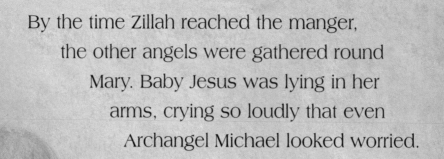

By the time Zillah reached the manger,
the other angels were gathered round
Mary. Baby Jesus was lying in her
arms, crying so loudly that even
Archangel Michael looked worried.

"What haven't we thought of?"
he fretted, as he gestured at all
the marvellous gifts that the
angels had brought. Before
Mary could answer, Zillah
hurled herself inside.

"Ah, Zillah! You've arrived after all,"
cried the Archangel Michael.
"And what have you brought
for the Son of God?"

Zillah held out the tiny blue blossom with petals like wings.

"Just a flower?" asked the Archangel. "That's hardly a proper gift for the King of Heaven and Earth."

But as he spoke, Mary took the flower from Zillah's hand, and the Baby Jesus stopped crying.

The angels were amazed.

"What do you call this flower of yours?" asked Mary.

"I don't know its name," Zillah said, softly. "But I found it growing in the snow and it gave me hope."

"Then that's what we'll call it," Mary smiled.
   "Hope. The greatest gift of all."